T0148012

From Love Child
to Hate Man

Vincent Mc.A Alleyne

iUniverse, Inc.
New York Bloomington

From Love Child to Hate Man

iUniverse books may be ordered through booksellers or by contacting:

iUniverse
1663 Liberty Drive
Bloomington, IN 47403
www.iuniverse.com
1-800-Authors (1-800-288-4677)

Because of the dynamic nature of the Internet, any Web
addresses or links contained in this book may have changed
since publication and may no longer be valid. The views
expressed in this work are solely those of the author and do
not necessarily reflect the views of the publisher, and the
publisher hereby disclaims any responsibility for them.

ISBN: 978-1-4502-2404-8 (sc)
ISBN: 978-1-4502-2405-5 (ebook)

Printed in the United States of America

iUniverse rev. date: 04/05/10

Contents

CHAPTER 1
The Beginning

Valerie Swift was born of a black woman and a white plantation owner. She inherited the nose of her father and her skin was neither white nor black, but of a light complexion. She would always be teased by her contemporaries of her looks. Many of them described her as a coconut; black on the outside but white on the inside. She felt she had not belonged to any particular race, the whites thought she was black and the blacks thought she was white. This caused her to be rebellious from an early age. She was tutored by her father who always felt that education was important and so Valerie learned to read and write at an early age.

This rebellion would cause her to give birth at an early age. By the time she was fifteen she was pregnant with Linda. Linda's dad was a much older man than Valerie and was a sergeant in the local police force. He had met

Valerie after she was arrested for disorderly conduct and he was captivated by this beautiful creation whose body had been referred to as a body of sin that would tempt anyone man or woman to indulge in illicit sex. Sergeant Jones was a tall handsome, charming man in his early forties who had lost his wife to the dreaded disease cancer and thought that he could never love again, that is until he had met Valerie who somewhat resembled his wife. In his opinion they both could have easily scored a 9.5 on his love scale of 1:10, 10 being the highest score. As Sergeant Jones got down to the business of questioning Valerie she looked at him and instead of responding she smiled. Her contagious smile will for evermore be etched in his mind as he too began to smile. This non-verbal communication said enough to bring these two lonely souls together. Their age difference was never a hindrance to what will later be regarded as a match made in heaven. There was only the problem of the difference in age and the likelihood that this law enforcement officer could be charged with carnal knowledge for getting involved in a relationship with a minor. This was the beginning of love affair that would end the career of the celebrated sergeant and the untimely death of a beautiful lady who had always gotten what ever she wanted in life.

The interview at the police station ended in a kiss on the wrist and a promise to see each other again. The promise became a reality the next day when the sergeant stopped by Valerie to see how she was doing. Valerie had taken the day off from school to relax following the incident the day before that ended in her detention at the police precinct.

As the sergeant arrived Valerie had just finished her bath with the beads of water dripping off her. She wrapped the towel around her and with effortless case walked her vivacious body towards the door and greeted the tall handsome Police officer clothed in the uniform of the local Police Force. As she approached him his eyes bulged as if they were going to pop out of his head and the perspiration fell off his face and drop on his uniform. His watery mouth wet his tongue and lips as he licked them in anticipation of a kiss, this time not on the wrist but on the golden lips of this young and beautiful teenager. As he embraced her she began to breathe loudly but this would soon be interrupted by two tongues rapping around each other with enormous passion. As one tongue melt against the other like butter on a warm summer day she felt the trill of sensation and the weakening of the knees. This was the sign that the officer did not come to arrest but to caress her and that the only prisoner she would be today would be a prisoner of love. He had not felt this way about a woman since the death of his wife; he had these feelings for a young girl who was twenty- nine years his junior and perhaps young enough to be his daughter.

This thought soon vanished from the sexual quarters of his brain as the sensation moved down his spinal cord to the genital area. This sensation caused a swelling in the immediately vicinity and produced a boom-like rod that was now the subject of attention.

As she felt this firmness against her wet body the wet towel dropped on the floor and revealed the remainder of the beautiful body that he had always imagined it to be. She could not help but notice the large bulge in his pants which she felt she had earned the God-given right to touch and feel, but her attempts to soften it by squeezing only made it firmer and harder. Suddenly she realized that they were not playing on a level playing field she was naked, but he was not and she began to viciously tear off the cloths of the local Police Force. Under normal circumstances he would have warned her that it was a criminal offence to destroy the uniform, but she had earned the legitimate right to strip him of his stripes. She pulled and toured the uniform until his tall slender body was exposed but still protected by the boom-like shaft which she continue to squeeze and stroke as it got harder and harder by every touch. As it began to heat up by static electricity she spat on it and sucked on it until it seemed to cool down a bit waiting in anticipation for the next stroke.

With a nod of the head and the pointing of a finger she motioned him to the sofa. He immediately responded with war-like haste and placed his head between her skinny but powerful legs. He too was in the business of providing lubricant to her clitoris that seems too to be running hot by the minute. He began to lick every square inch of her body with clinical precision as her young elastic body reacted spontaneously to every lick and every touch. In the last half an hour she had matured into the woman he always wanted to be the replacement for his wife.

She was over-excited she was running out of patience she needed to feel him inside her. From the size of his penis she knew it was going to hurt, but what was a little pain blended with pleasure in abundance. She was willing to take her chances with the hurt as she knew the pleasure would overcome the intermittent bouts of pain. She made up her mind she was finally ready as she guided his long hard penis to the point of penetration. She was now in the big league. Up to this point in time she was dealing with boys her own age that had barely pushed back the hymen but never penetrated. As his penis began to tear the hymen for the first time she associated sexual intercourse with pain. The pain was short lived as the pleasure took over as he stroked her with effortless ease to the shouts and rhythm of her body.

As he continued to stroke her with increased intensity the thought ran through his head that he could be discharged from the Police Force, but at this moment his mind was on another discharge which would come first. It was not long after that he ejaculated with laser like precision. She too had timed him well as they both reached a climax together.

CHAPTER 2
The Pregnancy

Almost immediately after the climax Valerie had a strange feeling come over her body. This was a feeling never felt before in all her fifteen years on earth. She was about to discover that this was not the only first. As the days went by, she began to feel nausea especially early in the mornings as soon as she got out of her bed. Her mother could not help but noticed changes in her behavior Valerie was acting strange and this usually quiet girl was becoming aggressive. She also noticed her regular visits to the bathroom and remembered her own situation when she was pregnant with Valerie. Could my daughter be pregnant? Who could have gotten her pregnant at such an early age? These are some of the many questions that flooded the head of Valerie's mother. It was time to investigate this matter.

She thought about telling Valerie's dad but at this point their relationship was still a big secret, after all he had his wife, who was already suspicious of the relationship they had. This was a battle she had to fight on her own at least for the time being. She had to approach Valerie to find out what was happening. Finally, she got the courage to approach Valerie as she sat her down on the sofa which was the centre of attraction a few weeks earlier.

In the meantime, Harry Jones was back at the precinct thinking about Valerie he had not heard or seen her after that day at the house. That day was as vivid as the day he walked through the door of her house. He had thought of it every day and every night since it happened. Had he done something wrong? Was it wrong to be in love with a fifteen year school girl? He had tried calling her every day since their encounter but had no luck. It was obvious that she was avoiding him but what for he could not understand. He thought of the consensual sex they had and total enjoyment and pleasure they both derived from it.

As he thought about it he felt that bulging in his underpants, a regular occurrence since that day. "Oh how I would like to see her now", he thought to him self. As he was thinking the telephone rang and a gentle but anxious voice asked to speak to Sergeant Jones. At first he thought it was the voice of Valerie, they were similarities in the pitch, but this was the voice of a more matured person. He acknowledged that he was Sergeant Harry Jones on the line. Valerie's mother responded, "I am Valerie's mother, could you come over and discuss an urgent matter?" "Was Valerie in trouble again," he inquired. Her stern voice echoed through the telephone line as she explained that she did not want to discuss the matter over the phone. "Okay madam, I will be there right away."

As he got up from his desk for the first time he realized the possibility that something was amiss. He felt nervousness in his chest as he drove towards the residence of Valerie. He was soon to find out his dilemma. Valerie was pregnant with his child.

He soon arrived at his destination which was ten minutes drive from the Police Station. He parked the Police vehicle and slowly walked towards the door. This time the journey seemed much longer than the previous occasion. There was no urgency in his steps, no great expectations only the same nervous heartbeat, this time with greater ferocity.

As he rang the door bell he heard the matured voice on the other side of the door as she walked toward the door. "I will be with you in a moment," she said. As she opened the door he could not help but notice Valerie sitting on the sofa, this time her skin color was pale and her smile was not as contagious as before, but still as inviting as usual. Valerie's mum directed him to a chair on the opposite side of the sofa with the appropriate distance between them that touching was not possible. Indeed the battle of words was about to begin.

Dorothy looked at him with great suspicion and contempt as she said in this calm and cold voice, "how long have you been sleeping with my daughter? Do you know she is a minor? Do you know that you can be charged with statutory rape?" As she was about to ask him to declare his intentions, Valerie interrupted, "mummy he did not rape me I love him and want to spend the balance of our lives together. Dorothy looked in amazement as they both spontaneously ran toward each other with open arms that matched perfectly as if they had belonged to each other. Harry tried to explain "I know that I am much older but with your permission I would like to marry her and care for her for the balance of my life. Dorothy nod in approval as she realized that these two persons were destined for each other, but the one thing Harry did not expect was the complaints from her silent father which would bring his conduct into question and his demise from the local Police Force.

No sooner than the matter was sorted out among Valerie, Dorothy and Harry the gossip began to make the beat throughout the force. It was not long before the Commissioner of Police summoned Sergeant Jones and demanded his resignation or faced disciplinary charges. Harry was a veteran of twenty-six years in the Police Force. He joined when he left secondary school at the age of eighteen. He knew no other job and he had no other skills. It would be difficult for a forty-four year man to start looking in the job market.

Harry had no choice, he did not want to cause any further embarrassment to his family or his new wife to be and their un-born child. The only asset he had accumulated was a second hand car and a small parcel of land that he inherited in the country side. As he pondered on how he could find gainful employment suddenly he realized that he could use his car to do taxi work and supplement if necessary by private security work, a field he felt at home with because of his experience in the Police Force.

His immediate attention was on his bride to be. He wanted to make her his wife as soon as was humanly possible. He had been married before and preferred a simple wedding, but would leave the planning to her because this was her first wedding, her big day, whatever she wanted to do was fine with him. She preferred a small wedding. All she wanted was to be with her husband to be, nothing else mattered. Eventually they would be married at a small ceremony at a small chapel in the village where he grew up. The ten people that attended were all close family and they all were happy for the newly married couple and their expected child to come. The next seven months of the pregnancy went well with Harry providing food and shelter for his wife. The taxi business was doing well and his occasional moon-lighting help to supplement the construction of a small home on the parcel of land in the country side.

The baby was born without any complications and she was named after Harry's mother Linda. Harry was the happiest man in the world. He always wanted children and Linda lived up to his expectations. She was a beautiful bouncing baby girl with a gorgeous face and long and slender body. Her blue eyes sparkle as she smiled; Linda Valerie Jones was the princess in the family.

Harry continued to work even harder to provide for his family and began to spend less and less time home with his young wife and his young baby girl. Harry found it extremely difficult to do two jobs and transport Valerie and Linda to Dorothy's place; so he purchased a small car for Valerie so that she could get around and do things for herself. Valerie soon realized that she was seeing less of Harry and begged him to spend more time with little Linda who was now two years and growing into a beautiful toddler. These long trips in the city to Dorothy's house would end in tragedy for the Jones' family.

CHAPTER 3
The Tragedy

It was a cold rainy night. The rain had been falling the whole day and Valerie and Linda had spent the entire day at Dorothy's house. They both fell asleep, but Valerie woke up at 11.30Pm and insisted on driving home. Dorothy begged Valerie to call Harry and explained that she had to spend the night because of the inclement weather, but Valerie had never slept away from her husband since they were marry and felt obliged to go home to her husband. As she was about to wake Linda her mother persuaded her to let her sleep until morning and she would bring her as soon as the rain held up. Valerie was reluctant at first but this would be the first opportunity in a long time that Harry and her would have spent together without listening in anticipation to the awakening cries of Linda. So eventually she gave in and headed for the country side.

Valerie left her mother's residence at 11.45 pm and she drove off and waved her mother goodbye not knowing that this would be last time they would be speaking to each other. The rain was pouring and the visibility was poor, it was only possible to see a few yards ahead of you at a time. As she drove along the way the trip that usually took an hour seemed to take forever. It was now 30 minutes into the strip and she had only managed to cover a quarter of the distance instead of half as is usual the case.

She continued on her journey imagining the precious time she and Harry will spend to night. It was almost twelve-thirty in the morning and Harry was usually home at this time. She search her hand bag for the cellular phone, but the battery was dead she had forgotten to charge it the night before. She had try calling Harry before she left her mother's home, but she did not reached him but she had left a voice message telling him that Linda was staying with her grandmother and that they would be spending the night alone and the plans she had for him when he got home.

In the meantime Harry had just arrived home and noticed that Valerie's car was missing from the driveway. Even though her car was not there he called out for Linda and Valerie hoping by some stretch of the imagination that they were both home. As he got into the house he called the cellular phone, but there was no reply and he left a message on her phone saying how much he love Linda and her at that to get home safe. As he sat down to take off his shoes he noticed that he had left his cellular phone at home and he observed the blinking red light indicating that he had messages. As he entered the voicemail box he heard the excitement in Valerie's voice as she was looking forward to spending the night together.

Harry immediately took off his cloths and headed for the shower as he waited in anticipation to spend some precious time with his wife. He reminisced on that day they had spent together at her mother's house and the eventual consummation of the wonderful relationship they had experienced together. He finished his shower lit two large candles, put on some classical music and waited in his birth day suit for the arrival of his beautiful bride. It was now 12.45pm and she could be expected any time now. It was just about an hour since she left her mother's house. He had called Dorothy and she confirmed that she had left at 11.45 pm and the hour strip would soon see the arrival of his young queen.

As Valerie glanced at her watch she realized that it was 12.45pm and that she should be arriving home in approximately fifteen minutes. The rain was still falling heavily and the visibility was even poorer. As she approached the dangerous corner over the bridge that divided a deep 100 foot gully a car came around the corner and headed straight at her and she was blinded by the bright lights. As she tried to avoid collision she broke the protective rails and as the car followed its trajectory into the ravine you could hear the screams fading away in the distance. The driver of the other vehicle suddenly stopped and realized what damaged he had done. He quickly called 911 and gave a description of the accident. He had managed to get a glance at the color and type car.

As the clock strike 2.00am Harry had nodded for a brief moment, the candles were almost down to the base, but there was no Valerie to be seen. He began to worry; she should have been home by now. He called her mother but she not heard or seen Valerie since she left her house. They began to worry even more as the minutes ticked away and there was no news of the whereabouts of Valerie.

They decided to hang up the phones and left the lines open in case someone was calling with news on Valerie. As Harry turned on the television set he heard the news that a white Toyota Corolla was involved in an accident and that the car had ended up in the deep gully. As a cold trill run down his spine he knew that the description fitted Valerie's car and that Valerie would have taken that road to get home.

He immediately got dressed and headed for the location. As he arrived outside was pitch black and the rescue team was trying to locate the car but the wet and slippery conditions made the operation impossible. Eventually they decided to abort the operation until it was day light. Harry however, could not wait until morning he knew if there was any chance of finding Valerie alive it would have to be now and he had to risk his own life in order to save hers. He borrowed the long rope from the rescue team and despite their pleading let himself down to the bottom of the ravine. His training as a police officer would serve him well as he lower his body to the bottom of the gully. As he reached the bottom he could see the white Toyota in the distance the lights still burning but there was no sign of life.

When he eventually reached bottom he rushed to the driver's seat of the car as the lifeless body of Valerie sat in the seat with blood all over her dress. She had broken her neck. There was a loud cry and shouts of Valerie you can't leave me. The rescue team realized that it was only the question of retrieving the body. A young life filled with potential had been lost. Harry had lost his beautiful wife; Linda had lost a wonderful mum and Dorothy had lost the only daughter she had.

The rescue team communicated to Harry to come up and they would deal with the matter, but Harry would have none of it he would spend the remainder of the morning holding the woman he loved so much in his arm for the very last time. He had promised to spend the night with her and he was not changing that promise for the world.

CHAPTER 4
The Single Parent

As Harry watched the coffin lowered into the ground he knew he would never love again. This was the second time that he had devoted his life to loving a woman and this is the second occasion God had taken the love of his love away from him. The only difference now was that he had part of her to remember him by. Linda was the splitting image of her mother and when she smiled Harry remembered the day he met Valerie, but that was all over; it was now time to raise his two year daughter.

Harry decided there and then that he would not let Linda out of his eye sight more time than was necessary. Dorothy volunteered to look after Linda but Harry felt it was his responsibility and he owed it to Valerie to raise their child the way they wanted to. It was going to be difficult. It meant Harry giving up one of his jobs if he were to spend the required time with Linda to make her the woman her mother wanted her to be. After considerable thought he decided to give up the security work and worked the taxi. This way he would be his own boss and would be able to devote the time to the raising of his daughter.

He enrolled her in a kindergarten School in the vicinity of the Taxi stand so that he would have been close to her in case of emergency. He had several offers for help from a variety of women who felt there was an opportunity to get a good husband but Harry was not interested in loving again. He never wanted to go through the pain of loosing a love one again. He would devote all his love and energy to his daughter Linda. He quickly learned to plait hair and do the other motherly things that are expected of a mother raising a young daughter. At first the plaits stood up in the air like horns much to the amusement of the other girls at the school, but Linda was quite happy to brag that her daddy had done the job and no one was going to adjust her hair. As far as she was concerned it was perfect and the other girls should ask their daddy to plait their hair instead of mummy.

There were times when Linda would ask when mummy was coming back but Harry would explain that she had gone to heaven and that some day both of them would join mummy in that wonderful place and they would be together for ever. Harry made sure that Linda attended church every Sunday as he wanted to instill the best moral values in his young child. As a police officer he had seen too many children hooked on drugs and destroyed the beautiful life they had ahead of them. He swore that he would never let that happened to his Linda.

For the most part Harry did a good job of being a single parent. He did, with some success, the things expected to be done by a woman in raising a daughter. Although he had a challenge of not knowing which rest room to take her to when she was too small to go by her self, most of the time he would take her into the lady's but was once caught and called a pervert by a female. He soon learned to wait outside and begged the ladies to do that delicate job for him.

Things were progressing smoothly with Harry he had done a wonderful job so far in raising his daughter. She was now five years and ready to go on to primary school. Harry, as predicted, found a school close to his work place to continue the tradition of protecting his daughter. He would take her to school every morning and be the first parent to collect on evenings. From there he took her home, he was finished working for the day, he would go home and make her dinner, help her with her home work before he put her to bed. This routine contentment soon got the better of Harry who began to remember the occasional drink he would take at the bar when he worked as a security guard at the night club. Oh how he craved for a drink, but he had given up drinking since that fatal accident his wife had. He had promised there and then that he would take care of his daughter. He could not bear the thought of his daughter losing the other parent. It was his responsibility to see her through until she could take care of herself.

As the years rolled on this routine contentment turned into total satisfaction, his daughter was now eighteen years and about to graduate from high school. The hard work had paid off she was a very intelligent student who graduated at the top of her class. It was now time to take care of daddy. He had spent the last sixteen years of his life making sure that she had the best education.

Linda knew that some day she would have to look for a husband and it was now time to get a woman back into her father's life. Her best friend, at school, father had died in similar circumstances to her mother and been raised by her mother as a single parent. The girls thought they were perfect for each other. They had planned the whole semester to get them together on graduation night. The rest was up to them. They were already acquaintances and had attended several school functions together, but never saw each other in the same light as the children. The children were already fraternal sisters and saw the transition to paternal sisters easy. The week of the gradation they planned to organize a romantic setting for their parents. First they had to prepare and groom their parents.

Linda started by telling her dad that it was time he started to love again and that she knew the perfect woman for him. It was her best friend Rosie mum. She was beautiful, kind and gentle and was already a familiar face in the household. Rosie had also launched her campaign of getting her mother to love Harry. Harry according to her was handsome, mature and a loving and caring father who was ripe for the picking.

They organized a dinner after the graduation ceremony for the four of them. The parents welcomed the idea that the four of them would be together not knowing that the plan was to have them alone to spend the time together.

They both planned a romantic setting at Harry's house because they felt that this is where he would be most comfortable. Rosie's mother Val was the out-going type and could be comfortable any where. The evening started out well with the family reflecting on the success of the children and the future that they would have ahead of them. Suddenly, the phone rang it was the girls' friend reminding them not to forget the graduation party. This party was a big secret up to this point in time. They both apologized to their parents for not remembering the party and asked for an excuse to attend. By now Harry and Val knew that they had been had. This was always the plan to get them together. They remembered the previous week of prepping, but what the heck they were already there and decided to enjoy each other's company.

As the classical music played and they watched the candle being blown by the soft and gentle breeze a smile came over both faces and simultaneously they both shook their heads in amazement. For the first time he realized how beautiful Val was. He had stopped looking at women in that vein and had promised not to love anyone again, but who said anything about love he was just there to enjoy Val's company and would take it one step at a time.

They got up from the table and with a simultaneous embrace and started to dance to the music of Beethoven. He had forgotten how it felt to hold a beautiful woman in his arms. She too had forgotten the fresh smell of cologne on a man's cheek. They realized that the room that was cold moments ago was beginning to get warm. The room was being heated up by the hot desire they had for each other. Neither of them was in this situation for a while but they would let their bodies dictate the next and subsequent moves. As they continued to dance the space between their bodies was decreasing, it was now zero. They felt their heartbeat in unison; they were both beating to the same drum.

He tried to pull her closer but she was already too close to advance any further as he felt the tips of her breast piercing his chest. The heart beat was getting nervously strong, his lips were vibrating and the lower part of her body was throbbing with sexual pain. As they eyes met she closed hers and patiently opened her mouth in anticipation of the long awaited kiss. It was several years since she had kissed a man intimately. As she closed her eyes she felt a cold tongue sandwiched between her lips, its target was her tongue and it reached its target it was greeted with a grip of pliers. She could still feel the throbbing of the clitoris as she transferred his hand to control the uncontrollable movement, but this exacerbated the situation. The hand did not work; it would take a specialist piece of equipment to fix the problem.

The equipment was pre-charged and ready to discharge its responsibility to the clitoris. In a flash he was on top of her and penetrating her with grace and precision. They both had forgotten what it was like to enjoy sexual intercourse. Yes indeed they had flashes of their late love ones making love but to night was theirs and nothing would stop them from enjoying it to the fullest.

Rosie and Linda had successfully completed their task it was now time to go to college and get on with their lives. This would be the first time they would be away from their parents for any considerable length of time. Linda was majoring in business and Rosie wanted to do medicine. They expect that some day they would return and make a contribution to their town. The next three years will be spent studying hard to reap the success and make the parents proud.

CHAPTER 5
The Love Affair

Linda and Rosie were roommates as expected at their new college and would spend the next three years together. At first they missed their parents and were wondering how the relationship was progressing. They had been successful in matching them together and it was now all up to the parents to consolidate the relation. Harry and Val continued to see each other and enjoyed each other's company but neither was interested in a permanent relationship. They spent most the time talking about their previous partners. Now that Harry was socializing again he began drinking alcohol again. He did not have his little girl to worry about any more.

This drinking got worse and Harry was involved in several accidents one of which was almost fatal. On that occasion Linda came back home and had to missed a week away from college. His relationship with Val was getting progressively worse until their decided to stop being intimate and go back being friends.

Back at school there were several boys that were interested in a relationship with Linda, but Linda seem to be attracted to older men and although she dated some the relationships never seemed to go any where. It seemed as though she was looking for someone to replace her daddy. She would find herself more and more attracted to her teachers instead of her contemporaries. There was particular teacher, Mr. Dick Browne that she had a big crush on. He was her lecturer in Business Statistics. Every time she had a class in Statistics she would tell Rosie how she would get butterflies in her stomach as soon as Mr. Browne walked into the class room. Mr. Browne was in his late forties married and had three children, two girls and a boy and seemed to be happily married.

Linda knew that she could not get involved with Mr. Browne. It would mean the end of his marriage and perhaps his career so she avoided him as much as was humanly possible. She prayed for the semester to over so that she could get out of the Business Statistics class. She was an "A" student and therefore needed no extra attention from Mr. Browne.

The three years went by rather quickly and both Linda and Rosie did well .They both received first class honors in their respective fields. Linda made sure that she avoided further contact with Mr. Browne by selecting electives accordingly. It was now time for graduation. Both Harry and Val attended the graduation and were proud parents of their children. Rosie and Linda decided to go back to their home town and make a contribution. Rosie did her internship at the local hospital while Linda took up a job in a junior management position at a government office.

Life back home for Linda was never the same there were frequent arguments with her dad about his drinking. His health deteriorating rapidly and he was in and out of the local hospital with kidney problems. Eventually, he died of kidney failure. Linda was now all alone. She was now twenty two and had lost both parents. She was very lonely and long for somebody to call her own.

It was not long before she found herself attracted to her boss at work. He was twenty-five years her senior, married and had two daughters. The eldest daughter was one year younger than Linda. Linda would work late at the request of her boss and soon realized that the attraction was mutual. Mr. Patrick Best was the Permanent Secretary in the Ministry of Industry and Commerce and always made compliments to Linda. At first they were genuine but as time went on these compliments changed to passes. He was very attracted to Linda and was willing to put his marriage on the line for her.

Mr. Best found himself working late every evening and would always request that Linda worked late as well. It was time to make his move. One evening while working late Linda intentionally picked something out of Mr. Best's hair and as soon as they made eye contact his tongue was down her throat. This would be the start to a love affair that was the talk of the town. Patrick was willing to make love to Linda, but she was in her menstruation cycle. That evening they kissed each other every part of each other's body. She placed her lips on his penis and he felt as if he was in heaven. In all his years dealing with women this was the only time he experienced such a feeling. He was anxious for the five day cycle to over so that he could finally make love to her. She continued to work late every evening and they continued to kiss and fondle each other. The period was over it was now time to go the full course. By now she realized that he would easily be aroused when she wore no patties so this became the order of the day. During the day she would come to his office and sit on the chair in front of him with her legs opened, without patties and invite him for a quick screw. Although she would arouse him sexually he was too scared to try anything during working hours. There was a constant flow of traffic in and out of his office and people in the office began to suspect that something was going on.

The evening had now arrived and it was now time to work late or so it would seem. The office closed at 4:30 and by 4:45 everyone had gone. It was only Patrick and Linda to do battle. As usual she teased him a bit by exposing herself without any patties. She spat on his penis and then licked it as if she had inherited this act from her mother. She placed it at the entrance of her vagina and then repeatedly took it out. By this time it at grown the full nine inches and was producing slime like an African snail. She convinced him that a condom was not necessary and so he obliged. She had sexual intercourse twice before but the three inches of penis she had was more like a tickler. This was the real thing and she was about to enjoyed the additional six inches that she was getting from Patrick.

She spent the next ten minutes sometimes moaning other times growing and occasionally begging for more. This is what she wanted all along an older man to love and protect her. She had finally gotten her father figure. The count down had begun; he warned her that he was getting there. She begged him to wait for her. He did and both of them climax together. Over the next two weeks this episode was repeated every evening. There was never a dull moment.

Four weeks had elapsed after her last period and there was no sign of a menstruation cycle. Like her mother before her Linda was pregnant for an older man. Patrick wanted to terminate the pregnancy. Her friend Rosie offered to terminate the child for her, but this was Linda's love child and she was not about to give it up.

CHAPTER 6
The Love Child

There was no way that Patrick or any one else could persuade Linda to get rid of her love child. Patrick was married, but she loved him tremendously and could not get rid of a part of him that was growing inside of her. Four months had past and all thoughts of abortion had vanished. It was time to look for a future for her child. She had to determine what role, if any, Patrick would play in their lives. She wanted Patrick to divorce his wife of twenty-six years and marry to her and raise they child. Patrick would have none of it. He could not separate himself from the family he loved so dearly, especially to his girls who meant the world to him. By this time rumors started to spread around the office that Linda was carrying Patrick's child. Eventually Patrick's wife would hear the rumor, but as far as Patrick was concerned it was just that, a rumor. The frequent meetings on evening begun to be reduced and after a while disappeared all together. Linda was doing all in her power to protect the life she had inside of her.

Patrick was under tremendous pressure in his household from his wife who initially was asking for a divorce, but she remained a housewife throughout the life of the marriage and could not afford the same life style as she was accustomed to. Her last daughter was only fourteen years old and required both parents in her life. Divorce seemed not to be an option in this matter.

There was never any doubt in Patrick's mind that Linda's child was his and he supported her during the pregnancy. Linda gave birth to a bouncing baby boy and she named him Jack Patrick Harry Jones. Jack was tall like his grand father Harry, but had his father's features. There was no doubt in Patrick's household that little Jack was Patrick's child. Jack two sisters adored him, but their mother wanted nothing to do with Jack. Jack was the son that she tried but never could have given Patrick and she was not about to lose Patrick to the younger Linda.

Linda was still on maternity leave and was seriously looking at giving up her job to take care of Jack, but she knew it would not be possible if she wanted to give Jack the life Harry had given her. She finally made up her mind that she would go back to work and employed a lady to look after Jack.

It was Patrick who suggested Kim. Kim was a lady in her fifties who never could have any children but whose husband got a son from a woman much younger than her. She was a long time friend of the family and Patrick thought she could be trusted to take care of his son. It was time to go back to work and Linda met with Kim and outlined what she expected of her.

Jack was now eight months old and the next ten years with Kim would determine what type of man he would become. Kim was in daily contact with Patrick's wife discussing the whole situation which was a constant reminder of her own situation where a younger lady got her love child from her husband who would eventually left her for the much younger lady.

It all started the very first day. Kim began her first day of torture to the young Jack. She left him in the cradle all day without feeding and when he cried she applied corporal punishment to get him to stop. Kim felt she had a responsibility to ensure that Jack would not grow up to be like Patrick or her former husband. She would ensure that he never had a liking for younger women when he got old. He would never put another woman through what she and Patrick's wife had to ensure.

CHAPTER 7
The Childhood

Kim decided to plan her strategy of raising Jack to mould him into the man that she wanted him to be. Over the next ten years Kim would teach Jack to hate young pretty women. She would buy the most beautiful Barbee dolls and showed him how to destroy them. Over the years she would have purchased several hundred Barbee dolls which he would have decapitated and buried them in Kim's back yard.

The relationship between Jack and his mother was bad initially but as she grew older they began to develop a good relationship. Jack was taught to love older women and as his mother got older he began to love her more and more and felt he had to protect her.

During the ten years that Kim raised Jack she purchased a large supply of dolls from China and continued the ritual of beheading the dolls at least twice a month. There were over one thousand dolls purchased by Kim for the exercise. Kim would sexually assault Jack from the time he was six years and would insist that one doll was placed between their bodies. After the act Jack then had to start this ritual of quarreling with the doll and begging profusely for the doll not to get between them. This episode would eventually end with Jack decapitating the doll and burying in the back yard. Jack would only bury the head but would keep the body as a souvenir.

Jack would spend the next four years under Kim sexual tutorage. Kim had no relatives and left her property in thrust for Jack when she died. When he reached eighteen years he would be the absolute owner of a piece of valuable real estate. The property consisted of the main residents and a cottage on two acres of land. It was inside the cottage that young Jack and the older Kim carried out the rituals at least twice a month.

Kim reported the daily progress to Patrick's wife until her death a year before Kim's death. They were both proud of the young man they were able to mould Jack into. Jack was never close to his two sisters. They were deliberately kept away from him. They never wanted him to express or feel love for a young person so his siblings were kept from him.

After Kim's death Jack became withdrawn and would spend eight years of his life buried in his books while he was in high school. He continued his trend of not dating girls his own age but would hit on his senior female teachers.

Oh how he missed Kim and would spend many hours of the day thinking of her and her sexual escapades.

He was attracted to his sixty year old History teacher. He would spend a lot of time seeking her attention. He was a grade "A" student in History.

He would request meetings with her just to be with her. Although he was an excellent history student he would encourage her to give him lessons just to be with her.

After several weeks of persuasion one day she decided to give him tuition after school. She lived alone since her husband had died. Mrs. Pile was a very attractive woman. She was a former beauty queen forty years ago, but still carried the grace and elegance of the former queen. Jack came to the house with the doll in his bag just in case he had succeeded in seducing her.

Mrs. Pile invited Jack in and offered him a seat. She inquired on what aspect of History he wanted to discuss. Jack stated that he had some queries about the American Revolution although he did an essay on the same topic and received an "A+". Jack never really wanted to do any History; he basically wanted to tell his-story of his attraction to older women. An attraction that led him to Mrs. Pile's house hoping that the attraction was mutual and that she could be to him what Kim was earlier in his life.

Mrs. Pile had previously notice that Jack had an attraction but dismissed it as the usual crush young men have on their older teachers. With time they disappear and with Jack she expected the same would happen, but she was wrong.

Jack sat down to tell his story   He   was   now eighteen years and has never dated a young lady his age, but finds himself more and more interested in older women. He spoke of his relationship with Kim and his feelings that he had for her. From the very first day he walked into her History class he fell deeply in love with her.

Jack looked more mature than his age; he had the looks and height of his grand father, Harry. He was only sixteen, but was already six feet tall. Mrs. Pile was taken by surprise, although she had suspected Jack's interest in her, but never thought for one moment that he would have approached her. She too was lonely and had not been with a man since her husband died. It was now six years since he had died and as much as she wanted to have a man in her life Jack was not that man, in fact she only considered him a child.

As Jack finished speaking to Mrs. Pile she could only counsel him. She had no intention of being the young man's lover, but recognized that he was abused by Kim and urgently needed help. She asked Jack to seek psychological counseling, but he bluntly refused and stormed out the door.

CHAPTER 8
The Adulthood

Jack would eventually drop out of Mrs. Pile's class and choose another elective and would spend the remaining years avoiding her. Jack remained secluded and would not mix with his peers. After the graduated from high school he enroll in the local college to study Forensic Science. He was in fascinated with mystery novels and spent a great deal of time reading novels and gathering information on DNA evidence. He also spent a considerable time reading his grand father's police reports on different crimes that had taken place during his stint as a police officer.

After graduation from high school Jack was able to acquire the property that Kim left for him. He was now eighteen years old and reached the aged of majority. Kim had also left him some money which was enough to support him during his years at college.

He was obsessed with his dolls and spent the next three years talking, crying and confiding in his life-long inanimate friends. His mother saw less and less of him and was rather concerned of his increasingly erratic behavior and suggested he sought psychiatric help. Jack however, felt that he was on top of his game and continued to live in his false world of dolls and dreams.

There were occasions when he tried to lure older women to his residence unsuccessfully. In one case he had managed to convinced one middle aged woman to visit. She visited on three occasions but on her last visit as Jack was about to make love to her she felt this strange presence and as Jack started his ritual with his doll she ran as fast as she could to get away from him and vowed never to return.

Jack continued his study of Forensic Science and his obsession of planning the perfect crime. He felt that with training, his knowledge of DNA and his twisted mind he would be able to plan the perfect crime and get away with it.

He wasn't about to try just yet. First he had to graduate from college and gained further knowledge in the field of Forensic Science that would enable him to plan the perfect crime. He continued to study hard and was once again graduated at the top of his class. Jack was now the holder of a Bachelor of Science degree in Forensic Science.

All was needed now was to get some working experience in his field of study. As was expected he joined the local Police Force following in the foot steps of his grand father and would spend the next several years working hard to make detective sergeant. It is there that he would excel in the field of gathering forensic evidence and solving many crimes. Jack however, remained a lonely man. There was no woman in his life although there were many offerings from several of his female colleagues.

Jack would remain steadfast and resolute in his decision not to get involve with younger women. He continued to treat with disgust older men who would have affairs with younger women and in the process cheated on their wives. He remembered the teachings too well from Kim and the conviction that it should never be tolerated.

One night while on patrol in the park he noticed an old gentleman parked out in a lover's lane with a much younger beautiful woman. She was very beautiful and reminded him so much of his Barbee dolls. Jack was not about to let this beautiful lass destroy another marriage. He had to stop this young lady from taking away the husband of a poor innocent old lady who was more than likely at home preparing supper for that criminal.

Jack quickly approached the car with his gun drawn. He quickly put the gun to the back of the gentleman's head and threatened to blow it off. He then demanded that the girl get dress and warned her not to let him see her in a similar situation again. Jack was so angry that he thought of killing both of them, but it was not in keeping with the well established practice of sexual intercourse and the doll ritual. Besides, the idea was to commit the perfect crime not to get caught.

Jack began to have mixed feelings about his role as a police officer. His role was to protect life and to ensure law and order, but this was conflicting with his beliefs that were instilled at an early age by Kim with the assistance of Mrs. Best. He would have visions of himself having sexual intercourse with younger women and the dream would always end with him beheading them and burying their bodies in the back yard and burning the head so that no one could identify the bodies. He would also ensure that there was no forensic evidence to link him to the crime.

These dreams would continue and would be repeated several times over, to the point where it was affecting Jack's performance on the job. The lack of sleep was having a serious impact on his judgment as a Police Officer. It was for this reason that Jack sought psychiatric help. This was recommended by his superior officer after he saw the decline in his performance.

Jack continued his erratic behavior and eventually had to be suspended from active duty while he sought further psychological evaluation. Jack actually beat a couple so badly that the older gentleman and the younger lady had to be hospitalized. This was a repeat of the incident that had occur before, this time he actually beat the couple for no apparent reason except his long believe that it was wrong for a younger woman to take away the husband of an older lady. The next several weeks would shape the future of Jack as a cop and a psychopath.

CHAPTER 9
The Psychotic Behavior

Jack was now visiting the psychiatrist three times a week, usually on Mondays, Wednesdays and Fridays. He would recall his battle of trying to be a successful police and at the same time having conflicting evil thoughts of beheading young beautiful girls. He had been given six moths off from work, after which his suitability for the Police Force would be determined. Jack was confused. He continued to have nightmares of his encounters with his assaults on young women. He would remember when a young female officer was given to him as his partner and the thoughts he had about killing her.

Initially a beautiful young psychiatrist was recommended to Jack. She had an excellent record of treating policemen, but Jack could not stand the thought of a young beautiful lady giving him advice. He opted for the much older Psychiatrist who he was comfortable with.

Jack continued his treatment three times a week, but no serious progress was made. Instead the frequency of the dreams increased and with each dream he was getting more and more violent.

He would use the remaining four days of the week to look for young ladies in lovers' lane in the park. He would particularly single out younger women with older partners and would continue to harass them pretending to be on active duty as a police officer.

It was now five months into the therapy and no significant progress was made. In a month's time Jack's future would be determined. He could not stand the thought of not being a policeman. He had studied, trained and worked hard to succeed as an officer and would continue the fight to get better. He tried extremely hard to get better, but it was if he was possessed by demons. They were taking over his life and his future. Jack was willing to try anything and everything to succeed. First he had a month to convince his superiors that he was fit to continue his work as a policeman.

Rumors began to circulate about his encounters in the park and this was not helping Jack's cause. He was warned to stay a way from the park or face immediate dismissal from the force. Jack managed to keep a low profile for the remaining month. Instead he would spend his time at home with his Chinese Barbee dolls. He seemed to be comfortable in the company of his dolls. It is the only time that Jack felt at home. It is the only time he felt he had a future.

It was now six months since Jack was attending therapy, but he was not ready to go back to work. This seemed to be the end of the line for Jack. His therapist however felt that she was beginning to break through with Jack. Jack was now beginning to feel more comfortable and was now confiding in her. He talked comfortably about his family history, his abuse from Kim and his inability to love women his own age.

As a result of this his psychiatrist recommended that the treatment be extended for a further six months. She felt that this would give her enough time to reach Jack and finally cure him once and for all. She advised Jack to start dating young ladies if he was to get over the hatred he had. Jack took her advise and started to see a young lady he had met sometime ago in the park. She was beautiful and Jack felt he could learn to love her, especially since she seemed to be a younger of Kim. He imagined that Kim looked exactly like her when she was young.

Jack seemed to be progressing well; he was more and more relaxed with his therapist and was more opened now than ever before. He even invited his new girlfriend to one of the session to see the progress he was making. He felt that if they were to trust each other that they would have to be honest about their dealings. It was now three months into the second session and Jack was making some significant progress. His dreams were less frequent and some nights he was not experiencing his nightmares.

In three months he would complete his session get marry and live the life he wanted as a policeman or so the thought. Jack continued to date his girlfriend, Ann. He even introduced her to his mother who he not seen for a long time. His mother was glad to see Jack happy. She had never seen Jack this happy before. She had only seen him smile like that before and that was on mornings when she used to drop him off by Kim in his early childhood. His girlfriend was happy also she thought that Jack was finally coming to grips with his situation. She was only waiting for him to pop the question and she would willingly accept.

It was now into the last month of the second phase of the therapy and his psychiatrist was very please with his progress. She had finally managed to reach Jack. She felt that Jack was ready to once again to take on his role as policeman and fulfill his obligation as a loving husband. Jack started to exercise once again. His was ready to take on his responsibility as detective sergeant once again.

The six months had now elapsed and the psychiatrist made a good recommendation to the commanding officer, Jack was now ready to rejoin his fellow officers. He had gone through a twelve month session and his dignity was restored. There was no reason why Jack could not function fully as a law enforcement officer.

Jack was welcomed back by his colleagues. He was an excellent officer and very efficient at solving crimes. His record was good. There were several unsolved cases that needed Jack's attention. His forensic experience was badly needed if the precinct was to enjoy the most productive station in the jurisdiction once again. It had not reached that status since Jack was on leave. Jack introduced his girlfriend to his fellow officers as his future bride. He was now ready and able to take on his role as officer and loving husband.

CHAPTER 10
The Hate Man

Jack had started back at work and had fitted right into the scheme of things as if a year had not elapsed. He was working harder than ever and reaping success. He had managed to solve several outstanding cases. He was now ready to take the next big step in his life. He was ready to be married and enjoy having a good family life.

Jack got married a month after his resumption of work. He had a few close friends and family. It was a quiet but nice wedding and the reception was held at Jack's residence. It was the first time that his colleagues had visited his home and they love it. Jack's trouble seemed now to be behind him.

His life had suddenly turned around and he was enjoying every moment of it.

On the wedding night as Jack consummated the marriage he had flashes of his sexual escapades with Kim.

She reminded him not to get involve with younger women. He began to sweat profusely and at times he was rough. This made his new wife enquire if something was wrong. Jack assured her that everything was in order, but that he was a little nervous not being with a woman for such a long time. However, he managed to reach a climax.

That night Jack could not get to sleep after having sexual intercourse with his wife. It was as if twelve months of treatment had gone down the drain. He tried calling his therapist but she was not available.

Jack had brought home a file from the station and decided to immerse himself into it. Eventually he went to sleep but had to face the challenges of the new day. He thought that he had been cured but his problems of the past was about to affect his future and that of his bride.

Jack went to work the next morning feeling down. He contacted his therapist and explained to her what had happened. He asked her in confidence not to report the matter to his superiors. She told him that she was no longer working for the Police and that he was protected by patient to doctor privileges. Jack organized a session once a week and although he did not tell his wife what had happened, he told his wife that he was seeing his therapist for follow up sessions.

Jack tried to keep himself busy at work and would work late into the night and would spend less and less time at home with his wife. Even on his off days he would find an excuse to be on the job. He was avoiding having sexual intercourse with his wife. He had repeated dreams of making love to his wife but it would always end with him beheading her and getting rid of the body. Jack was really in love with his wife and did not want to harm her. This is why he was trying desperately to avoid the physical contact with her. The demonic forces were at work pushing Kim's wishes to destroy his beautiful bride. He would not let this happened; he would commit suicide before he took the life of his loving and beautiful bride. He would rather offer the souls of other young girls, but not that of his beautiful bride.

Jack was warned by his boss that he was working too hard and demanded that he took his off days. Jack did not want to spend the time at home and would spend a lot of time in the park reading at first and then exercising afterwards. He continued his fascination with mystery novels and plotting the perfect murder. He was obsessed once again with the idea that he could get away with a carefully planned murder.

He would run for hours in the park and when he was finished he would watch the couples come into the park and make love. He was particularly interested in the relationships of older married men cheating on their wives with younger women. He decided that he would now occupy his time investigating these couples to ensure that the older men were married and in fact were cheating on their wives. This would be his new found job on his off days; to investigate such cases and put an end to this disgusting trend.

Jack once again began to feel the hatred that Kim had thought him to exercise with younger women. It had to stop. He was not going to allow the older wives to suffer like how Kim and Mrs. Best's wife had suffered at the hands of beautiful younger women. He remembered the story that Kim had told him about his mother putting herself between Mr. and Mrs. Best and began again to hate his mother. The idea that he was a love child was getting the best of him and the idea of committing suicide would continue to occupy his mind.

He would continue to go to therapy and discussed the issues with his psychiatrist. He would tell her about his feelings about committing suicide and the hatred he had for younger girls and how he felt about being a love child. He was advised by his therapist to confront his mother and explain to her how he felt if he were to get over this hatred and his feelings to commit suicide.

Jack would visit his mother later that afternoon and confront her as his psychiatrist as recommended. For the first time his mother had seen the psychological damage inflicted on her son by both Kim and Mrs. Best. She had left her young son in the care of a woman that she felt, on the advice of her lover, was capable of raising him. Instead she brain-wash him and had produced a monster of a man. She always knew that her son was a little strange, but never knew what had caused the behavioral change in the young man. She blamed herself for bringing a love child into this world. She should have taken the advice from her friend Rosie and her then lover Mr. Best to abort the infant, but instead he brought a child into this world that was made into psychopath.

She began to recap an incident that happened when Jack was only six years old when he told her that all young women were no good and wanted killing. At that time she could not get him to open up, but now he had confronted her she realized that this is the time Kim had started to abuse him.

This is perhaps the first time that she really had regrets about giving birth to the love child. She tried to console Jack pointing out to him that he was a good man and that God had put him down here for a purpose and that not all young beautiful women were evil. He had a beautiful wife who was a good person. Jack suddenly remembered that he had not heard from his wife all day and stormed out the house and went home to his wife.

As he drove home he began to weigh his options; should he tell his wife how he really feels about young women or should he continue in a relationship that turned out to be a lie? He felt that he might get up one night from one of his dreams and hurt his beautiful bride. She was the exception, yes she was young, she was beautiful but above all she was faithful and had no intentions of leaving Jack for an old man.

For a moment he would put his evil thoughts aside and go home and hold his beautiful wife in his arms and relate to her how much he loved her. As Jack arrived home his beautiful wife was waiting at the door for him. She ran out and embraced him and told him how much she had missed him all day. She gave him a passionate kiss which apparently put all evil thoughts out of Jack's head, at least momentarily.

That evening Jack and his wife had a great romantic time together. They enjoyed the dinner his wife had prepared and ate under candle light to the sounds of classical music and a taste of red wine. Jack had not made love to his wife since the night of the honeymoon and he was eager more than ever to do so. As they retired to bed Jack and his wife began to make love. For the first five minutes it was beautiful. It was passionate and it was meaningful. His wife was feeling comfortable and began to experiment. She began to have oral sex to Jack. This was the first time Jack had experienced oral sex and although it was good he remembered he was thought by his sexual teacher Kim and it was dirty and that only whores do it. Suddenly, Jack felt a lump of hate moving from his genital area through his throat to his brain. His head was now swelling with hatred. He began once again to have flashes of the abuse from Kim. He was angry and begged his wife to stop. He pushed her away and stormed out of the room. She called after him inquiring what was wrong, but he headed for the comfort of the cottage where his idol dolls awaited him where he locked himself in until the next morning.

The next morning Jack went over to the main house as if nothing had happened the previous night. His wife sought an explanation as to what went wrong, but Jack assured her that everything was fine as he kissed her and went off to work.

On his way to work he contacted his therapist and explained to her how he had confronted his mother and while it worked initially eventually he had a bout of the same hatred as he was making love to his wife. She asked Jack to come in for a session later that evening where he would explain the anger he has and his desire to do evil things. He told the therapist that evening that he would kill himself, but the only thing was preventing him from doing so was the fact that he felt obliged to first rid the world of those wicked young girls. He was not going to let them destroyed any more marriages.

CHAPTER 11
The Victims

Jack continued to have his dreams. It was now affecting his ability to function as a detective in the local Police force. He was no longer the crack detective he used to be. He would work for long hours but would not see the result. He habitually turned up late for work. His partner did not wish to work with him any longer because he had put his life in danger. No one wanted to work with him any more. Every day Jack was beginning to be more of a liability than an asset to the force.

His superiors were made aware of Jack's continued therapy with the psychiatrist and sought an official report of his suitability to continue his work with the force. At first the psychiatrist did not want to provide the information because she knew that the report would not be Jack's favor, however when the Chief ordered Jack to see another therapist, Jack agreed that the report should be made available to the Force. This was the beginning of the end to Jack's career as a police officer. There was no more time available for treatment. Jack had already been given a year to recover from his depression.

The report was made available to the Chief of Police and it was decided to take Jack to the Medical Board.

Jack knew that once he was placed before the Medical Board that he would be dismissed so he decided to submit his resignation instead. The resignation was to take effect a month from the day it was submitted by Jack but instead Jack was paid a month's salary and asked to vacate office immediately.

Within the first week of Jack being home the relationship with his wife got progressively worse. Jack had more time on his hand to dream his even thoughts. He was no longer relating to his wife. He began to inflict both metal and physical abuse on her. He confessed that he had never really loved her and that he used her to see if he could have gotten over his dislike for younger women. She became more and more scared for her life and decided to leave Jack before he actually carryout the treats to behead her.

Jack was now a free man again. He was now able to carryout his rituals with his dolls without detection. He would continue to experience the strangest of dreams. This time he was not controlled by his presence in the law forces. He was no longer an officer of the law so he was not obliged to be lawful in his dealings any more.

He missed his job as an officer so he eventually applied and received a license to operate as a Private Investigator. His specialty was the investigation of partners who cheated on their spouses, especially women who cheated with other people husbands. This gave him the authority to be a "Peeping Tom" whether or not it was legitimate to do so. Although Jack was now employed he found time to think evil thoughts. He would spend hours in the park peeping behind couples and would follow them home to determine their place of residence. He would use his influence to gather information on couples to determine whether or not they were cheating on their partners.

Jack was hired by an elderly lady to investigate if her husband was cheating on her. The lady gave Jack the facts; she was concerned that her husband was getting home much later than usual and spending a great deal of time away from home. Jack was delighted to take this case. This was the type of case that was of particular interest to Jack. It fitted perfectly into the Kim's model of a young lady trying to take away an elderly gentleman from an old lady. Jack could not ask for a better opportunity, a case that not only provided monetary rewards but personal satisfaction.

Denis Paul was a man in his mid sixties and had is owned law firm. His wife Sally has always been a faithful wife and had helped Denis to build a successful law practice. Sally spend her early days working for the firm, first as a legal secretary and then as the office manager before her retirement when she was sixty. It was five years since her retirement and she noticed behavioral changes in her husband. He stopped enjoying spending times with her. He would come home early on evenings and have walks around the block.

One evening Denis got home unusually late and she noticed some red lipsticks on his white shirt and when she enquired about it he made up some excuse that his secretary accidentally bump into him. This along with the fact that he was coming home later and usually too tired to have sex made her suspicious and felt the need for a thorough investigation. She could not have chosen a better Private Investigator than Jack. It was right up his stream.

Denis had recently hired a young lady from out of town. She was a beautiful twenty year old lass with long dark hair, a slimly built body and lovely breast. She was Denis new secretary and was hired perhaps for her looks more than any thing else. She had beauty but lack brains and her typing skills were below that of a ten year old child, but what she lack in brains she made up for in looks. Denis did not mind her inefficiency as a secretary after all he had two other secretaries that could do the work. She was hired to be his show piece and not his work horse.

Denis gave new meaning to the word Laptop. It moved from a portable PC to his secretary Pam sitting on top of his lap every day. The only thing in common the Laptops had were the strokes that "de keys" made.

It was now Jack's responsibility to find out what was going on between Denis and Pam, but his responsibility went beyond Mrs. Paul requirements. He also had to satisfy the requirements of his long time partner in crime Kim to ensure that Pam never had the opportunity to take away Mrs. Paul's husband.

Jack parked outside the law office of Mr. Paul and waited for Pam and Dennis Paul to emerge. Jack was now waiting two hours and there was no sign of the couple. Jack was beginning to think that they were making love inside, but he had no way of knowing if this was really happening. He could not take the chance of getting too close to the building. The security guard was outside paying careful attention to the surroundings so Jack had no choice to patiently wait until Pam and Denis exit the building. There was no chance that they were inside doing any thing. The office was still heavily populated. He contemplated, then reasoned that they were waiting for outside to get darker. It was that time of the year in the Southern Caribbean when the sun set early. It was now six-thirty in the evening and outside was beginning to get dark. Suddenly Pam and Denis appeared at the door. They were both smiling as he motioned her to his car parked at the back in the lone garage. Jack was good at following without detection. He spent most of his years as a detective performing this role.

As Denis drove out of the drive way Pam took off her jacket and made her self comfortable. Jack was not about to loose them. He wanted to know by the end of the evening what was going on between Denis and Pam.

It was now dark as evident by the on-coming car lights. It was now thirty minutes since Denis and his partner left the office as they traveled along the coast road to a small hotel on the East Coast of the island. Jack parked in the car park while Pam remained behind. He went up to the front desk and collected a key for room 69. From what Jack could see through the glass door Denis was a regular at the hotel. All indications were that he was familiar with the setting as he laughed and joked with the attendant.

Jack remained in his car until Denis came for Pam and took her up to the room with the balcony over-looking the sea. On the balcony Denis started to kiss Pam as he held her in his arms. It was a moon-lit night and the ray of light lit up the blue calm waters of the shore. Jack got caught up in the moment he too was feeling sexy as evident by the bulge in his pants. Denis would continue to kiss and fondle Pam until she was ready with anticipation to go inside.

Jack got out of the car and went to the front desk and persuaded the desk clerk to give him a room on the balcony. He got the Room 68 which was next to Room 69.

As Jack entered the room he could hear Pam screaming for more and telling Denis how he was the sweetest man she ever had. Jack continued to listen to the squeaks of the bed as it was moving to the rhythm of the reggae music playing on the radio. It was Bob Marley's "one love". Jack sat on the bed and listened until there was no song from the squeaking bed. The radio had stopped paying Bob Marley and was now playing Percy Sledge's "Take time to know her." There were no other songs emanating from the room. For a moment Jack thought that they had left the room. To make sure, he looked outside and could see Denis's car the same place he had parked it. He then heard a whisper from Pam, "Did you enjoy me?" Denis responded, "Of course I did." The couple would spend the next hour relaxing and chatting. It was now time to head back down the road. Jack had gotten the evidence he came for. All was required now to find out where Pam was living and his task would be completed.

Jack followed the couple as Denis drove for forty-five minutes to Pam residence. It was a lovely single family residence in a quiet sub urban area. It was obvious that Pam could not afford a house like this on her own. It came with the compliments of Denis.

As Denis drove away Jack contemplated his next move. He was mad and did not want to report his findings to Mrs. Paul but he knew he had to break up the relationship. He got out of his car and went up to the house and ran the door bell. As Pam answered he convinced her that he was friend of Denis and that he was in the neighborhood and he asked him to look in on her.

Pam did not think twice, anyone who is a friend of Denis is certainly a friend of hers. She opened the door and Jack forced himself in. He told her how Denis's wife had hired him to investigate the relationship between her and Denis. He advised her that he would like her to stop seeing Denis and he would simply tell Mrs. Paul that there was nothing going on between them and hopefully once she is out of the picture then Denis would go back to his life with his wife.

Pam would have none of it. She was furious to the point where she asked Jack to leave. She was not about to give up a life that she never had. She left her poor house and was desparate for a better life and was not about to give it up without a fight.

Jack was extremely angry; he heard the words of Kim ring in his ears "don't let that young whore take away that lovely old lady husband." Jack gave her one slap which knocked her unconscious to the floor. Jack realized that there was no way he could persuade Pam to leave Denis alone. He picked her up from the floor, made sure that there were no witnesses and placed her in his car and headed for his home.

By the time he arrived at his home she was still unconscious. He placed her in the cottage and proceeded to dress her in Kim's cloths, put on makeup to make her looked a lot older that she actually was, handcuffed her to the bed and began to rape her. During the ordeal Pam became conscious and began to scream but no one could hear her but Jack threatened her that he would kill her if she didn't stop. Jack would eventually gag and began the ritual he had gone through so many times with Kim and his Chinese dolls. He would continue to rape her for the next forty-five minutes and while doing so he would place a doll between them and repeatedly throw it to the ground begging it not to get between them. This is the first time since the death of Kim that Jack felt at home with a woman.

As Jack finished raping Pam he knew there was no turning back now. He had to get rid of her. Besides, she was a perfect stranger out of town so the only person that knew where she lived and would miss her was Denis. Jack first had to take off the makeup and old fashioned cloths to make Kim looked young again. He could not take her life dressed like Kim. To him he would be killing Kim and all she stood for. That was not about to happened. Jack took off the cloths and cleaned her skin of the several layers of makeup that made her looked old. When he finished she was the beautiful young body that he brought to his residence. He was now ready to get rid of her once and for all.

Jack placed his large hand around her small neck. His hand surrounded her entire neck as he began to choke her. She remained gagged, but begged with her eyes as she muttered for mercy. She gasped her final breath as her lifeless body slumped into Jack's arm. It was now all over Jack had three-fold satisfaction. He had satisfied the requirements of Mrs. Paul. He had given great satisfaction to Kim and his own satisfaction of ridding society of a whore who was destined to break up a wonderful marriage.

It was now time to complete the ritual. This time there was no substitute doll Jack had to fulfill his dream of decapitating a real head. He went to the kitchen got a large knife and slowly removed Pam's head with the precision of a surgeon. He carefully ensured that there was no DNA evidence left behind. He proceeded to also cut off the head of the Barbee doll, burned the real head of his victim and buried the doll with the ashes in his back yard. It was now time to get rid of the real body.

Jack would spend the next week disposing the body in fine parcels in several states a considerable distance from his home town. After the week had passed Jack returned to his home town and reported to Mrs. Paul that there was no evidence to support her claim that Paul was seeing a younger woman. Paul could not understand why Pam would disappear without letting him know that she was doing so. Everything at the law firm soon went back to normal. One of the older secretaries got a much needed promotion and became Denis secretary and things in the household went back to normal. Jack had satisfied his desire to kill. He had successfully claimed his first victim. There was no turning back; he would repeat the routine again and again.

Jack would continue to frequent lovers' lanes looking for young people who he suspected were having affairs with older married men. He would investigate them thoroughly, find out where they lived and then would do whatever was necessary to eradicate them from the face of this earth. It was now four weeks since his first victim. He remembered that his ritual called for at least two victims a month. It was now time for his second victim.

Jack would spend his time frequenting bars looking for young beautiful women. He would follow them home and investigate their circumstances. He wanted to make sure that when he made his move that there were no relatives to report that the persons were missing. He wanted his victims to live alone, single and more important he wanting them to be young adulterers. Jack was not about to be caught now. He had hundreds of dolls awaiting his executions. There was one doll for each victim so he had a long way to go.

It was a Friday night and the bar was packed to capacity and there were two young ladies next to Jack talking. Jack overheard the younger one Jane saying that she was involved with this marry man several years her senior and that she would ensure that he left his wife for her. Jack pricked his ear and listened attentively. She would be perfect for his ritual. All was required now to complete the profile was that she had to live alone.

Jack spent the remainder of the evening watching every move the young lady made. That night she drank profusely and was in no position to drive home. Her girlfriend offered to take her. Jack became agitated that Jane was not driving home herself. He was blood thirsty for a next victim but from his training as a Police he knew that the chances of getting caught were greater if a witness was present. He pondered for a while; should he do the double? It was getting close to the end of the month and he only had one victim to show for his hard work and now he had the opportunity to have an extra one for the month which meant that he did not had to work quite as hard.

As the young ladies exited the bar Jack quickly followed behind. Jane's friend put her in her car and went over to check that Jane's car was alright. Jack in typical Police fashion recorded both car numbers. He may not be in a position to score tonight, but for future reference he would add the names to his database. As the young ladies left the car park Jack followed them to Jane's house. It was situated about five miles from the bar in a spacious subdivision of one acre lots. The area was not fully developed and there were only two houses completed included the one in which Jane was residing. Her married partner was a developer and had constructed this house unknown to his wife.

Jack waited outside in anticipation like a lion perched for a great kill. He could smell the rawness of human blood in his nostrils. He repeated his thoughts over and over again should he give Jane's friend time to leave or should he move in right away for the kill? After all he was a trained police and had dealt with many dangerous situations. He could easily over-power these two individuals and kill two birds with one stone. He waited patiently as he watched the light in what he assumed was the bedroom went out. As he was about to exit his car he noticed an oncoming light. He lowered his head in the seat so that he would remain unnoticed. This suddenly made up his mind; he was not going to take any chances. He would wait for another opportunity. He drove away regretting that he had not scored that night.

As Jack reached home he began to ponder on the night's events and sulked for not achieving his goals. As he reflected he reached for one of his Barbee and cried himself to sleep. The next day he would awake with Jane and her friend on his mind. He could not wait for night fall to have another chance at either one or both of them. During this time he would carryout his investigation which revealed that Jane had no family in town and was having an affair with a married man. This fit perfectly within the parameters of his plan. All was required now was the great catch. In his investigation he also discovered that Jane was not employed. Her lover did not wish her to work. She was given a car, a house and five thousand dollars spending money each month. She spent most of her days relaxing or shopping with the Platinum Visa card her lover provided.

Jack followed her around for a whole week planning when would be the best time to make his move. The week went by and the chance never prevented itself. Jack had to wait until Friday night where she was a regular at the bar. This time her friend was not present. They had planned to meet that night, but she called to say something came up and she was unable to meet. This would not prevent Jane from having a good time. Jack chatted briefly with her but made sure he was not seen leaving with her. He announced that he was leaving for the night as if he was cementing his alibi just in case she had to be missing then no one would say that she was seen leaving with him. There was no need to follow her any more. He knew exactly where she lived. He had done his home work and her lover was out of town on business so the course was cleared.

Jack left the bar and droved to Jane house and waited for her. He waited for about an hour before she arrived. As she parked her car and moved towards the entrance Jack came out from behind the heavily planted area with a handkerchief filled with chloroform. He grabbed her from behind and placed the handkerchief over her nose and she became unconscious immediately. He then placed her in the trunk of his car and headed for the doll mansion.

There he would perform the ritual like before, dressing her to look like an elderly lady, having raping her almost lifeless body and eventually beheading her. As in the case of the first victim he burned the head and buried the ashes with the Barbee doll that had accompanied both of them in bed. In usual fashion he would spend the next week getting rid of the finely cut body parts in several states. Jack had satisfied his quota for the month. In a few days it would be the beginning of a new month and he would need to seek new victims.

Over the next ten years Jack would continue to carryout his rituals. He branched out into different towns with a minimum of two victims a month, but some months when the opportunity presented itself he would kill four young ladies. When he was in different towns he would keep the ashes and get rid of the body parts the same way but made sure that the ashes and the head of the doll was buried in his back yard as an offering to the previous owner, Kim. In the decade he would have killed over three hundred ladies and was running out of dolls and back yard space.

Jack was also beginning to take chances. This was something that he had not done before, but he became more and more obsessed with the idea of the perfect crime and the success he had achieved for over a decade. One night when he was on one of his missions he murdered a young lady after having sex. This time he decided to take the body home to perform the ritual. This was unusual since in such cases he would get rid of the body and only take the ashes along with the doll to be buried in his yard.

Jack had to dive sixty miles back to his home town. He was tired and as he approached his home town about a mile from his residence he fell asleep and struck a wall and was injured badly. Jack became unconscious and was taken to the local hospital where he remained unconscious for two weeks. In the meantime the local police could not wait for him to become conscious to explain why he was driving around with a body with the head completely severed from the body. Along side of the body the police also noticed the head of a Barbee doll and several other dolls in the trunk of his car. They also noticed bottles of chloroform in the trunk of the car. There was also the smell of chloroform on the body as well as on the hands of

Jack. This was enough evidence to merit a search warrant to search Jack's residence.

Jack regained consciousness and was questioned by the police about having a headless body in his car. All of a sudden Jack had amnesia and could not even remember who he was. In fact he could not even remember his fellow officers or nothing about the accident and what had taken place. The police however managed to get a search warrant and went to Jack's house where their discovered hundreds of headless dolls buried in ashes. There was no forensic evidence at the scene to implicate Jack in the rest of the murders. The Police had no bodies and it was not against the law to cut off the head of a doll.

The police would eventually charged Jack for the murder of the woman in his car. The police had a theory that Jack had killed several women and burned their bodies and buried the ashes with the heads of the dolls, but although this was strong circumstantial evidence, it was not enough to get a conviction. The police would eventually charged Jack for the murder of Jill White, the woman found in his car. Jill was from out of town. She was a primary school teacher and was missing for the last three weeks. It was only after her picture appeared on television that her family came forward and identified her. Jill was the Jack's typical victim. She was young, beautiful and was having an affair with and older married man. Jack remained in prison and awaited his trial.

CHAPTER 12
The Trial

Jack's mother hired the best attorney money could buy and the trial began five months after the accident. By this time Jack had fully recovered from the accident but although his claim that he was suffering from amnesia he recognized his mother and remember some incidents that had occurred in his childhood. However, his doctor was satisfied that it was possible to have gaps in memory in such cases. Medical reports however suggested that Jack was fit to stand trial.

The prosecution case was built on the strong evidence that Jack had murdered Jill White and was taking her body back to his residence to burn it and to bury the ashes with the headless doll that they found in the car. They suggested that Jack used his knowledge as a forensic expert in the police force to get rid of all evidence to implicate him in what they suspected were hundreds of bodies murdered over time and represented by the number of headless dolls found in Jack's back yard. The emphasis was not on those bodies however, it was on the body found in Jack's car and that was the only murder they needed to prove that Jack was guilty of.

The defense would argue that there was no evidence to suggest that there were other murders at least only murders of dolls which could have been there before Jack inherited the house from Kim. In fact the defense had evidence to support the fact that the dolls were purchased by Kim from China. In relation to the body they would argue that Jack had spent a considerable time away from his car and since the car was not locked it was possible for anyone to put the body in Jack's car without his knowledge. With respect to the chloroform Jack would argue that he was conducting an experience to see how much of the substance he could use before becoming unconscious. The defense would further argue that on the morning in question Jack carried out such an experiment and that is why the chloroform was still on his hand.

The trial lasted two months at which several witnesses were called by both the defense and the prosecution. The prosecution called the psychiatrist that had earlier treated Jack who indicated that he was capable of committing the crime. The defense strongly objected to this evidence indicating that it should be stricken from the record because of doctor to patient privileges. The prosecution would rebut arguing that the doctor was qualified to give an opinion on the matter since she had several interviews after the incident had occurred.

The defense would also bring they own expert witness who would argue that Jack was incapable of murder. He had spent several years protecting life and upholding law and order in the society.

After the prosecution closed their case it was time for Jack to take the stand in his own defense. The defense questioned Jack on his outstanding record as a police officer and the many murderers he had solved in his time. He also told the jury how on several occasions Jack had put himself in danger to protect others. On one occasion he was even shot and almost succumbed to his injuries. "Was this a man capable of murder?' he enquired of the court.

It was time now for the prosecution to cross-examined Jack. They would use the opportunity to question Jack on his own dealings with women. Why was it that he did not like young women? They asked him his feelings on women cheating on their husbands. This question seemed to have struck a hatred note in Jack's brain and he showed his anger in court. That was enough to convince the jury that Jack was capable of violence and he was not the sweet innocent lad that the defense was purporting him to be. Jack was the final witness on the stand and it was now left to the twelve member jury to determine the fait of Jack.

The jury made up of five women and seven men deliberated for two days and would later return a verdict of guilty of the murder of Jill White. Jack luck had finally come to an end. It was time for the judge to summon the jury back to the court room. As he asked the foreman of the jury, "Foreman of the jury what is your verdict? As jack stood there he felt the nervousness trickled down his body and he slowly heard the words of the foreman. "We the members of the jury found the defendant guilty as charge for the murder of Jill White. The decision was unanimous 12 to 0. All the members were in agreement that Jack had committed the heinous crime of murder. As the Judge thank the jury and dismissed them, Jack remained speechless for the very first time he understood the wrong he had committed. His lawyer whispered across in his ear," we will appeal". Jack would have none of it. He did the crime now he had to spend the time.

The judge made his announcement, "Jack Jones you have been found guilty of the murder of Jill White for which you will be sentence to death by the electric chair. May the Lord have mercy on your soul". Tears ran down Jack's cheek but he was too guilty and shame to cry aloud. Finally he would be at peace with himself. His mother sobbed loudly and wondered where she went wrong. The thoughts ran through Jack's head he had fulfill Kim's wishes for ten years. The only regret was that he did not train anyone to carry on.

CHAPTER 13
The Sentence

Jack was rushed off to maximum security prison and as he was rushed out of the court house he could hear his mother crying loudly in the background. He glanced at her and gave her a smile perhaps reminding her that she started it all when she had her love child from a marry man. He was no longer her love child he had grown into a hate man. It was all her fault.

Jack would spend the next six months in maximum security awaiting his execution. During these six months he would face many challenges from fellow inmates; they were people that he had put there for all types of crime including murder. Some of them, like Jack, were awaiting execution and would try to kill Jack before his official execution. To Jack it did not matter if he was killed by their hands or the electric chair. He had come to an understanding that he had to pay for the crimes he had committed. For the first time in his life he no longer felt guilty, he was sleeping peaceful at night. There were no more nightmares, no dolls to worry about and no more rituals to follow.

He found one friend in prison who was in for armed robbery and was proud of Jack's work. Jack would confide in him and give the details of all the murders he had committed. Ron was very interested and although he had no chance of leaving that institution he wished he could duplicate the events of Jack's life.

As Jack was taking his daily exercise one day he was attacked by an inmate that he had captured in solving one of his many murder cases. He was stabbed with a make-shift knife made out of a spoon. Jack was rushed to the local hospital in a critical condition. He would spend the next eights weeks recuperating from his injuries only to be made ready for his execution. Jack wished that his fellow inmate had killed him but he was not that lucky. He still had a date with the chair which he had no choice but to keep.

He was now all alone Ron was attacked in the same incident and had succumb to his injuries. The inmate responsible was executed while Jack was in the hospital. Jack would spend the remaining three months lonely awaiting his execution. It was the longest wait in his life. The hours felt like days, the days like months and the months like years. The wait was long and Jack was getting inpatient he thought about taking his own life, but he was a brave soldier and wanted to face the music up front for

73

the many people he had killed. He was proudly referred by his fellow inmates as Jack the ripper number 2.

The day had finally come. That morning the priest came and Counsel Jack, but he had done his own preparation. He was ready to leave this earth and join his dear friend and lover Kim. There were a few witnesses to the event. The priest was on hand and two other prison officials. The day before his mother had requested to see him but Jack had refused.

Jack smiled as he sat in the chair. The official asked him if he wanted to be blind-folded, but Jack refused. He wanted his witnesses to see that he took it like a true warrior. He was not scared nor was he going to beg for mercy like some of his victims. The operator asked Jack if he had any final words before the execution. Jack smiled and would only say let's get on with it. Those would be Jack's last word as a sizzling sound came from the chair and a puff of smoke polluted the air. When the smoke had cleared Jack's lifeless body crouched in the chair. It was all over Jack had kept his date with the executioner.

The End